The Magical Adventures of Ayden and Dawn

Ayden and The Dancing Trees

By Tammy Paro

DEDICATION

To my brother, Kyle Olson, for your unconditional love,
depth of compassion,
insight and infinite belief in me.
I Love You.

On one bright Sunday morning Ayden jumped out of bed, as parade of questions marched 'round in his head.

Today was the day that he'd longed for all week. Nona had a surprise she said nothing could beat!

He put on his slippers, first his left, then his right. Then he pulled up his bedspread and turned out his light.

Ayden was hoping that Dawn was awake, not asleep, as their Nona had told him she had not yet turned three. So he pushed the door slowly, as to not make a peep, but his sister had heard that one little squeak.

As she turned 'round to face him she was
smiling real big, and held out her arms while
still clutching her pig.

The piggy was something called a Puffalump. It had started out cuddly, but was now filled with lumps. The lumps didn't seem to matter to Dawn, for wherever she went, that pig went along.

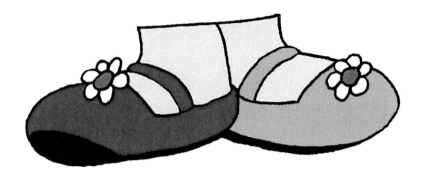

Ayden helped Dawn get down off her bed. He put on her slippers: one lilac, one red. Her left foot wore lilac and red for her right. When she looked down and saw them, she squealed with delight!

Ayden got a warm feeling whenever he helped her. Either big things or small things, did not seem to matter. He wasn't sure what he felt deep inside. Nona had explained that the feeling was pride. Pride, she had said, was a powerful tool and it helped us remember to follow the rules.

Dawn took his hand and off the two went, and to get to the kitchen they followed the scent. Dawn guessed it was pancakes and Ayden, french toast. But as it turned out, Nona had made them both.

Each chair had a cushion different from the rest, and Ayden had always liked his the best. Dawn's cushion had animals found on a farm, Ayden's had robots with really long arms. Nona's cushion was green and covered with stars. Mom's cushion had butterflies, and their father's had cars.

After eating is clean up, and then time for chores. Dirty clothes in the hamper and no toys on the floor. But then, don't forget, there's still one thing more.

Nona explained it was dental hygiene, but Ayden and Dawn called it teeth sparkling clean! They hummed to the tune of the ABC's twice, and each checked the other to be sure they looked nice.

They both ran off excited and quickly got dressed. Dawn did it all by herself and Ayden was impressed. Everything matched and her shoes were on right. Ayden just checked that her laces were tight.

Ayden tied both of his sneakers and put on his jacket. Nona helped Dawn because she didn't know how yet. When they'd all gotten ready, they went out the back door. Nona held both their hands 'cause that's what hands were for.

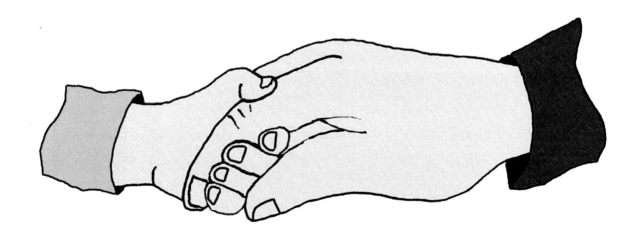

They were both buckled into their car seats, just so. Nona put on her seat belt and said "Here we go."

As they drove past the houses on Tumbleweed Lane, Nona said that, "Surprises aren't always the same. There are some you can hold and some you can keep." When I looked at my sister, she'd fallen asleep. Nona said, "Mother Nature's surprises are clever, even if you can't hold them, you can keep them forever."

As they climbed from the car the first thing he could see, was that in every direction, there were nothing but trees.

And then Ayden asked, "Can we please see our surprise?" Nona said, "There are things not just seen with our eyes. We use other senses and that's part of the magic." Then she bent down and zippered up Dawn's light pink jacket.

They walked down the stone pathway between lots of trees and his sister's pink hat got pulled off by the breeze.

It went lickety-split like a kite on a string. Nona grabbed it so fast he did not see a thing. It was flying away and, the next thing he knew, it was back on Dawn's head, just a wrinkle or two.

As they entered the clearing Ayden thought at last, here was the surprise and it would be a blast. There in the clearing was a park filled with children and a sandbox and swings and a slide and small buildings.

The both of them started to jump up and down, and Nona smiled sweetly and said, "Run along. This is not your surprise but you'll have lots of fun, your surprise will come later, now go on, run along."

They made sand castles and motes and when they were done, they headed right to the swings because flying was fun.

Dawn was too small to use the same swings as Ayden, but Nona was right there to help solve that problem. Nona put her into a swing made for children her size and she pushed her and he wasn't even surprised.

He thought deep in his heart, that his Nona had magic, she knew what to do when she hadn't been asked yet.

After they played for what seemed like forever, Nona called them both over for snacks and some water. She cleaned both their hands with some little wet wipes, and they all sat together in the warm bright sunlight.

When their snacks had been finished, the trash put in the bin, Nona said, "Come on you two, it's time for my plan. The sun is exactly where it needs to be and your surprise is close by, let's go sit by those trees."

She took both our hands, as she most often did, and we walked toward a tree trunk that was really quite big. The closer I got the more I could see that the trunk was a bench that had been carved from a tree.

They all sat on the bench and he thought it was neat, that the really old tree trunk, made a nice comfy seat.

Nona said, "Okay children, let's all close our eyes. The sounds all around are part of the surprise."

The first thing he noticed was the strange rustling sound, and then he recalled there were leaves all around. Then Nona asked what he felt on his skin, it took him a second and he told her, "The wind." Right then Nona said, "You can open your eyes, because standing before you is your surprise!"

They opened their eyes and nothing was there, then Dawn looked up at Nona and simply asked, "Where?" Nona got right down on her knees, and with them both beside her, she said, "Look at the trees."

"If you look you'll see they're dancing, as their branches swish and sway. It's like a celebration and it's happening every day. There's a music made by nature and it's carried on the breeze, and although we can not hear it, it is still heard by the trees."

Ayden turned slowly in a circle, and could not believe his eyes - he could see the trees were dancing, what a magical surprise!

Then he looked over at his sister, her little arms in the air, and while holding tight to piggy, she danced without a care.

Nona wasn't spinning, but she had a beautiful smile. She said, "I've been waiting to show you for a while. It's why I always tell you to see things with your heart. The world is filled with magic, and these trees are just the start!"

As we made the drive back home, I realized she had been right. It was like in the darkness you saw things one way, and then you turn on a light.

THE END

35492780R00030

Made in the USA
San Bernardino, CA
26 June 2016